#1294

Little Critter's®
THIS IS MY FRIEND

BY MERCER MAYER

To Eric Christensen

A Golden Book • New York
Western Publishing Company, Inc., Racine, Wisconsin 53404

This is my friend.
My friend is special.

I like to surprise my friend.

My friend and I talk
to each other
every day.

Sometimes my friend
does not like
what I say.

Sometimes I do not like
what my friend says.

Sometimes my friend
gives me things.
Today she gives me
a cookie.

I like cookies.
But this one is weird.

This cookie
is made of sand!
Yuck!

My friend thinks
this is funny.
I do not think
this is funny.

I try to tell
my friend that.
But my friend has
someplace to go.

Sometimes my friend
makes me mad.

Sometimes I make
my friend mad.

But I give her
some flowers.

My friend likes flowers.

Sometimes I fall down.
I hurt my arm!

My friend makes me
feel better.

A spider scares us.

But I am brave.
"Go away!
Do not scare my friend.
My friend is special,"
I say.

My friend shares with me.
That makes me happy.

I take a lick.
I take a bite.

I like ice cream.
It is so good.

My friend even
gives me the cone.

Sometimes I wait for
my friend.
I like to surprise my friend.

Sometimes I give
my friend things.
Now I give her
a present.

She opens the box.

"What is it?"
she asks.
"It is a rock,"
I say.
"It is my favorite rock."

"Thank you,"
says my friend.
She gives me a kiss.

My friend and I
give each other
many things.

But friendship is
the best there is.